For Scarlet who is just right to hug
and Beccy, her lovely mom ~ S.S.

For K, with love and hugs ~ C.B.

LITTLE TIGER PRESS
1 The Coda Centre, 189 Munster Road, London SW6 6AW
www.littletiger.co.uk
First published in Great Britain 2010
This edition published 2013

Too Hot to Hug!

Steve Smallman

Cee Biscoe

On the coldest day of a cold, cold winter, Ryan was high in the mountains, searching for firewood.

His fingers were blue.

His nose was purple.

And he still hadn't found a single stick!

Then, through the swirling snow,
he saw a **cave**.
"It looks **warm** in there," he thought.
"Maybe there's a fire!" So he went inside . . .

There wasn't a fire, just a big, golden egg.
And it was HOT, hot-water bottle hot!

Ryan picked the egg up, and felt its warmth

spread from his nose to his toes.

"Ahhh," he sighed.

Then he thought of his poor mom and dad in their freezing cottage. He put the egg in his basket and hurried home.

"Look what I found!" said Ryan.
"What is it?" asked Mom.
"WARM!" said Dad, and he smiled for the first time that week!
But just then . . .

Tap!

Tap!

CRACK!

...out hatched a **baby fire dragon!**

"Wow!" said Ryan.
"Ooh!" said Mom.
"No, no, NO!" cried Dad. "NO dragons!
They're nothing but trouble! You'll have to take
it back RIGHT NOW!"

The baby dragon blinked and sniffled.
His bottom lip wobbled, and he
began to cry.

"Hush," said Ryan. "Don't cry."
And he gave the little dragon
a BIG hug.
  "Ooh! He's as warm as
toasted crumpets," gasped Ryan.
"You try, Mom."

So Mom hugged the dragon. Even **Dad** hugged the dragon.

"Can we keep him, Dad?" asked Ryan.

"We can call him Crumpet!"

All through the winter, Crumpet the dragon kept the family warm and snug.

He **dried** the laundry.

He **warmed** the beds.

He even **made the toast!**

But the **hugs** were the **best!**
And everywhere that Ryan
went, Crumpet went too . . .

. . . except on **bath night**. Ryan **hated** bath night. The water was always cold, and Mom made him wash behind his ears where his favorite dirt was.

Crumpet was **scared** of water, so he hid behind the sofa making worried squeaky noises until Ryan was dry and the water had gone.

Then he **hugged** him until he was
warm and toasty.

Soon, winter turned to spring.
The snow started to melt.
Flowers bloomed, and Crumpet
started **to grow.**

And as he grew, he got . . .

HOTTER!

"It's boiling in here," groaned Dad.
"GO AWAY, CRUMPET!"

Crumpet went over to Mom for a hug.
"OUCH!" yelled Mom. "You're too HOT to hug!"

Ryan hugged Crumpet, but it wasn't warm and snuggly anymore. It was hot and scorchy.

Then one day, Crumpet burned the toast, scorched the laundry, and set fire to Mom's best bedspread.

"THAT'S IT!"
shouted Mom and Dad.
"CRUMPET HAS
TO GO!"

Early the next morning, Ryan and Crumpet set off up the mountain. By now, Crumpet was so hot that his feet left little scorchy footprints in the grass.

Even through his glove, Ryan's fingers felt very hot as Crumpet clung to his hand.

Then, as they reached the bridge, Crumpet saw the water and gripped Ryan's hand even **tighter**.

"OWWWWWW!"

Crumpet slipped backward
and fell into the water,

WHEE,

PLOP,

HISS!

"CRUMPET!" yelled Ryan,
but Crumpet had disappeared
in a cloud of steam.

Ryan jumped in to save him
from the cold, mountain river . . .

But the water **wasn't** cold, it was lovely and **warm**! And there was Crumpet, splashing and gurgling and giggling.

Ryan hugged him tight. And it wasn't hot and scorchy anymore—it was toasty warm again. The cold water had cooled Crumpet down!

"That's better," said Ryan. "Let's go home."

And from that day on, Crumpet the dragon lived happily with Ryan and his family. And now whenever Crumpet gets too hot to hug . . .

...he has a great, big
bubble bath!